Rabbit and Fox

Written by Jill Eggleton
Illustrated by Paul Könye

PEARSON

Rabbit went in the hole.

Fox looked at Rabbit.

"Come here," said Fox.
"Here is a carrot."

"Too little!"
said Rabbit.
"I like **big** carrots."

7

Fox got a **big** carrot.

"Here is a **big** carrot,"
said Fox.
"Come here!"

"Too little!"
said Rabbit.
"I like **big, big** carrots!"

10

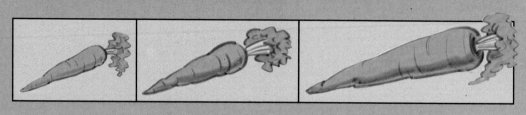

Fox got a **big, big** carrot.

12

"Here is a **big, big** carrot,"
said Fox.
"Come here!"

"Look!" said Rabbit.
"I am here.
 I am in **this** hole!"

A Map

Key

garden

hole

trees

▰▰▰ Guide Notes

Title: Rabbit and Fox
Stage: Early (1) – Red

Genre: Fiction
Approach: Guided Reading
Processes: Thinking Critically, Exploring Language, Processing Information
Written and Visual Focus: Map, Speech Bubbles
Word Count: 75

THINKING CRITICALLY
(sample questions)
- What do you think this story could be about?
- Look at the title and read it to the children.
- Why do you think Fox wanted to give Rabbit the carrot?
- Why do you think Rabbit kept sending Fox away for bigger carrots?
- How do you think Fox felt when he saw that Rabbit had tricked him?
- What do you think Fox could do next to try and get Rabbit?

EXPLORING LANGUAGE

Terminology
Title, cover, illustrations, author, illustrator

Vocabulary
Interest words: hole, Rabbit, Fox, carrot
High-frequency words: looked, little, too
Positional word: in

Print Conventions
Capital letter for sentence beginnings and names (**R**abbit, **F**ox), full stops, commas, quotation marks, exclamation marks